Clever Climbers

Jill McDougall

Contents

Animals That Climb

Lots of animals are very good at climbing.

Some animals need to climb to get food.

Tree frogs climb trees to catch insects. Some goats climb trees for food, too!

This tree frog eats insects in trees.

These goats climb trees to eat the fruit.

Other animals need to climb
to stay safe.

Sometimes, bear cubs climb trees
to hide from hungry, bigger bears.

Ants

Lots of insects are clever climbers.

Ants are very good at climbing. They have tiny claws at the ends of their legs to help them climb.

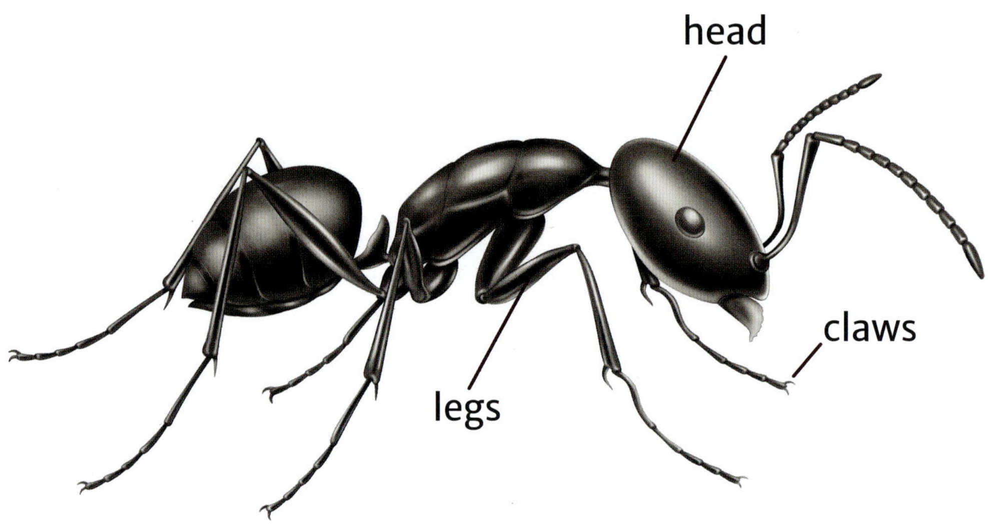

Ants can climb up walls to get into buildings. Sometimes, they look for a warm place to make a nest.

Some ants climb up and down trees. They build their nests in the treetops.

These ants have built a nest with leaves.

Stick Insects

Stick insects are insects
that look like little sticks.

They have claws on their feet
to help them climb.

Stick insects hide in trees and eat leaves.
They can walk upside down on branches!

When it is windy, stick insects sometimes
fall off the branches,
but they quickly climb up again.

Geckos

Geckos are small reptiles that can climb very well.

Sometimes, they live inside houses. They run up and down the walls to catch insects.

Geckos have five toes on each foot.
Each toe has lots of tiny hairs
that help them stick to walls and windows.

Snakes

Snakes are reptiles that can climb along fences and over big rocks.

Some snakes can climb
up the sides of houses!

Sometimes, snakes climb trees to catch birds
or take eggs from nests.

Snakes do not have legs to help them climb.
They pull their bodies up
with the help of their **scales**.

Leopards

Some big cats are very good
at climbing.
Leopards are big cats
that can climb trees.

Leopards have very sharp claws.
They grip the tree hard
with their claws
to pull themselves up.

Sometimes, leopards take their food into a tree to eat it.

On hot days, they rest in trees to stay cool.

Lots of animals are clever climbers.

They climb up and down to find food, stay safe or make a new home.

Glossary

scales tiny, hard parts of skin on the outside of a snake's body

tree frogs frogs that live in trees